Hearts & Crafts

Sheri Brownrigg

TRICYCLE PRESS
Berkeley, California

To Mom and Dad
With Love.

———————————

TRICYCLE PRESS
P.O. Box 7123
Berkeley, California 94707

Illustrations by Sheri Brownrigg
Book design by Tasha Hall
Cover design by Tasha Hall and Sheri Brownrigg

Library of Congress Cataloging-in-Publication Data
Brownrigg, Sheri
    Hearts and crafts / by Sheri Brownrigg.
        p.   cm.
    Includes index.
    ISBN 1–883672–28–7
        1. Handicraft—Juvenile literature. 2. Heart in art—Juvenile literature.
3. Wearable art—Juvenile literature. 4. Valentine decorations—Juvenile literature. 5. Valentine cookery—Juvenile literature. [1. Handicraft. 2. Heart
in art. 3. Clothing and dress. 4. Valentine decorations. 5. Cookery.] I. Title.
TT160.B857   1995
745.5—dc20   95–12079
                                                                                    CIP
                                                                                    AC

First Tricycle Press printing, 1996
Printed in Canada
1 2 3 4 5 6 7 8 — 01 00 99 98 97 96

Contents

Contents

Acknowledgments

Special thanks to David Hoehn, Mary Robinson, and Robin Oldham who each let me borrow a craft or a quote.

Every effort has been made to trace the ownership of all copyrighted material and to secure the necessary permissions to reprint these selections.

"Each friend…" by Anaïs Nin. From *I Call Thee Friend* by Arlene Hamilton Stewart, copyright 1993 by Smallwood and Stewart, Inc. Reprinted by permission of the Publisher.

"What do…" by Haley Wadsworth. From *American Girl,* February 1995. Reprinted by permission of Pleasant Company Publications.

"The Rose Family," by Robert Frost. From *The Poetry of Robert Frost,* edited by Edward Connery Lathem. Copyright 1928, 1969 by Holt, Rinehart and Winston. Copyright 1956 by Robert Frost.

Introduction

My favorite day of the year has always been Valentine's Day. A day set aside for exchanging the symbols of love is the best excuse for a holiday. Anticipating beautiful flowers, boxes of chocolates, and lacy cards is sweet suspense. Add your own creative gifts to this show of love, and life seems pretty wonderful indeed. But, of course, the meaning of Valentine's Day and the fulfillment of pampering yourself and your loved-ones with homemade crafts do not have to be tied solely to February 14. Kindness to yourself and to others is always in season.

Look at the world through rose-colored glasses. Conquer the perfect heart. Write love letters with a tulip pen and seal them with a kiss. Brew up a tea party and invite your friends to eat the table decorations. It's difficult to think negative thoughts while making a tiny pig holding a flower!

Most importantly, take your time with these projects and *enjoy* yourself. Time well spent is the sweetest gift of all.

Safety First!

Some of the projects in *Hearts & Crafts* require the use of an oven, a sharp blade, a glue gun, or permanent markers. Young children should always be supervised by an adult; there is no substitute for taking one's time and taking care.

Always read all instructions before beginning a craft. Assemble your materials, and set up a suitable work surface. I've suggested using aluminum foil in working with Sculpey™, spreading out newspapers when using paints, markers, and glues, and using cardboard under anything being cut with an X-acto knife.

Sharp blades (X-acto knife, knives, scissors): When an X-acto knife is called for, it should only be used by an adult. When other sharp blades are used, adult supervision is necessary.

Nails and needles: Keep nails and needles in a special place so they will not be dropped on the floor and possibly stepped on. Never put these in your mouth. Take care when using these to poke holes in things.

Kitchen oven and stoves (including a double-boiler and toaster ovens): Use only with adult supervision. Adults should review general kitchen rules before children use these items.

Hand mixer: When using a hand mixer, make sure the bowl you are mixing in is securely placed on a flat work surface such as a kitchen counter. Keep hair, clothes, and kitchen towels out of the way of the rotating blades.

Special Materials

Sculpey™: This is a new kind of polymer clay. There are several other kinds of polymer clay which can be substituted, like Fimo, but I have found Sculpey™ to be the easiest to work with. Be sure your hands and work surface are clean when working with Sculpey™. You can bake it at 275°F on a glass baking dish in a regular kitchen oven or in a toaster oven. An adult should assist in putting items in to bake, taking items out of the oven, and making sure they are cool enough to touch. Most items require ten to fifteen minutes of baking. Note of caution: unbaked Sculpey™ can stain fabrics.

Glue: For crafts made of fabric, use a fabric glue. Suggestions are Aleene's "tacky" glue or FABRITAC. For crafts made with paper, cardstock, and cardboard, use white school glue. For plastics, ceramics, and other materials, use a low temperature glue gun.

Low temperature glue gun: Available at art, craft, and hardware stores. This is an electric tool that holds a stick of glue. It heats the glue so you can shoot it out by squeezing the handle. The great thing about a glue gun is that the glue dries very quickly and it holds really well. Although I recommend a low temperature gun, please take care not to burn yourself.

Mod Podge: This is a glaze you can use to give a nice coating to your craft. It is easily found at most craft stores, but you can also substitute white school glue (like Elmer's Glue-All) as a glaze. Always use glaze with an adult in a well-ventilated area.

Cardstock: You can find this at arts and craft stores. This is a heavy paper similar to the kind commercial greeting cards are made of. You can substitute construction paper if you wish.

Foam craft: This is brightly colored material that is actually a thin sheet of foam. It's available at most craft stores. If you cannot find it, substitute cardstock or construction paper.

Conversation hearts: These are small candies in the shape of hearts that have messages printed on the top of them like "hot dog," "you're cool," and "be mine." They come in different sizes, the most common size being about ½" from top to bottom. The larger size is about 1". You can find these at drug stores or candy shops.

Craft stick: Available at craft stores, these are wooden sticks with one pointed end. The point makes a good tool for poking holes in things or even for sculpting clay. They come in different lengths, but they are also easy to break to desired lengths.

Shapes and Symbols

SYMBOLS
Wonderful images taken from folklore have come to represent kind wishes. Use these symbols in your crafts, or come up with your own secret code:

Heart	*love*
Hand	*friendship, or extending help*
Sun	*joy, life*
Cup	*abundance*
Dove	*bearer of message (usually of love or peace)*

Cupid	*playful love*
Angel	*protection*

FLOWERS

Try communicating through flowers. Here are just a few flowers and their unspoken meanings:

Rose, tulip	*love*
Jonquil	*return my affection*
Orchid	*thoughts*
Daisy	*innocence*
Gardenia	*love in secret*
Violet	*shyness*
Lavender	*calmness*

COLORS

Colors can affect our feelings and even our actions. Changing the color of your shirt can change your mood for the day. These colors are great to use in crafts that are made for showing love:

Red	*warmth and feeling*
White	*faith, purity, peace*
Pink	*delicacy*
Purple	*passion*

NUMBERS

Do you have a lucky number that has special meaning for you? These numbers are good for sweethearts:

1	*favorite; two become as one, or "we are one"*
2	*couple; also the month that Valentine's Day is in*
9	*love potion number nine is the strongest one*
14	*the date of Valentine's Day*
16	*the sweetest age that a girl can be*
64	*from the song by the Beatles, "When I'm Sixty-Four"*

WRITING WITH NUMBERS AND SYMBOLS

Translation: Be My Love Today

Patterns

Several crafts in this book require tracing patterns or creating reusable patterns. Here are step-by-step instructions for both of these:

TRANSFER PATTERNS

You Will Need:
>   Tracing paper
>   Pencil
>   Paper or cardstock

How to Transfer Patterns Directly to Paper or Cardstock:
1. Lay tracing paper over the image you want to replicate.
2. Use a pencil and trace over the line of the image.
3. Lift tracing to see if all lines have been copied. If not, replace tracing paper and trace any missed areas.
4. Turn tracing paper over on flat surface and shade along the underneath side of the lines you have drawn. Shading is easily done by holding the pencil at an angle and rubbing back and forth.
5. Turn tracing paper over again, with the shading on the bottom, and place on paper or cardstock where you want to have the image.

6. With pencil, draw on top of the lines you first made of the image. The charcoal from the shading on the underside will transfer to the paper or cardstock.

7. Remove tracing paper and refine the new image by darkening where necessary.

REUSABLE PATTERNS (STENCILS)

You Will Need:
    Tracing paper
    Pencil
    Scissors
    Cardstock

How to Make and Use Reusable Patterns:

1. Replicate an image on cardstock by following the previous instructions for transferring patterns directly to paper or cardstock.

2. Cut out the newly made image.

3. Trace around the pattern on whatever it is that requires an image.

4. Save your new pattern to reuse.

Perfect Heart Pattern

I have to tell you about the time I taught a four-year-old boy to fold and cut paper hearts. It was as if he had

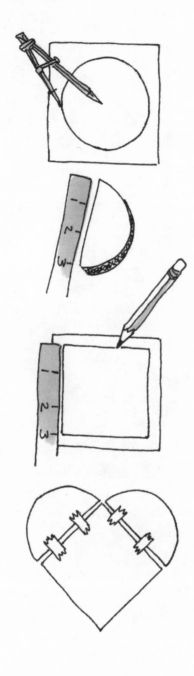

learned magic. He was so pleased, and not just for himself, but because he had already decided that the hearts he made were for his mom, dad, and sister. It was then that I realized we have a natural desire to make and give hearts.

Here's an easy way to make a perfect looking heart.

You Will Need:
   Compass
   Paper
   Scissors
   Ruler
   Pencil
   Scotch tape

How to Make:
1. Use a compass and draw a circle on a piece of paper.
2. Cut the circle out and fold it in half.
3. Measure the folded edge. Use this measurement and make a square with the sides the same length as the measurement of the folded edge on the circle.
4. Cut the circle in half on the folded edge.
5. Tape half the circle on one of the square's edges and the other half on an edge just next to it. Perfect.

Fun and Loose Heart Patterns

When a perfect, traditional, symmetrical heart is not what you are looking for, try some of these unusual, whimsical shapes in your crafts.

It is only with the heart that one can see rightly. What is essential is invisible to the eye.

—FROM *The Little Prince*, BY ANTOINE DE SAINT-EXUPERY

❦ CHAPTER 1 ❦

Wearable Art

What better way to display your creativity than to become a walking gallery and wear your jewelry and accessory pieces.

Conversation Heart Barrette

I have always loved the conversation hearts sold before Valentine's Day, but they are difficult to find at other times. This craft and the one following will allow you to have these sweet little words with you whenever you wish. Save a few hearts to munch on.

You Will Need:
> Pastel colored cardstock cut 1" x 3½"
> Scissors
> Hair clip backing, ⅜" x 3"
> Piece of aluminum foil about 10" square
> Low temperature glue gun
> 32 small conversation hearts
> Small bottle of Mod Podge
> ½" paint brush

How to Make:
1. With the scissors, round the corners of the cardstock piece.
2. Place clip, top side up, on the foil.
3. Center the cardstock to clip and glue with glue gun.
4. Glue a first layer of 17 hearts on cardstock.
5. Then glue twelve hearts on top of the first layer.

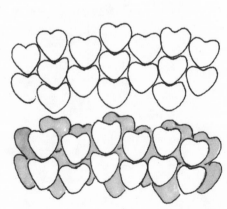

6. Glue three hearts across the middle of the second layer.
7. Paint with Mod Podge and let dry.

Conversation Heart Necklace

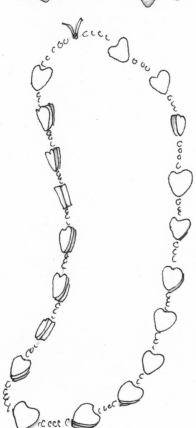

You Will Need:
    2' white kite string, dental floss, or jewelry thread
    38 conversation hearts
    Threading needle (optional)
    108 ⅛" or 2 mm plastic pastel beads (optional)
    Low temperature glue gun
    Mod Podge
    ½" paint brush

How to Make:
1. Lay a heart under the center of the string, with the blank side facing the string.
2. Glue the blank side of another heart to the back of the first heart, making sure the string is between the two hearts.
3. Leave 1" of string between the hearts, or, as an option, thread 6 beads on each side of the hearts. Repeat steps 2–3 until satisfied.
4. Tie a knot with the loose ends of the string.
5. Paint the hearts with Mod Podge and let dry.

The heart speaks every language.

—THE AUTHOR

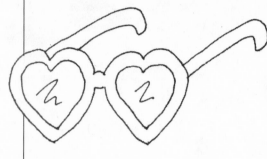

Rose-Colored Glasses

It has been said that the world looks better through rose-colored glasses. It is my guess that it looks even better if the glasses are heart-shaped.

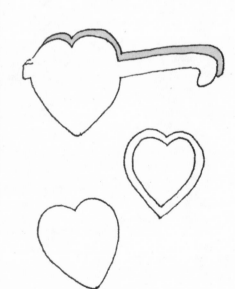

You Will Need:
> Tracing paper
> Pencil
> Cardstock
> Scissors
> 18" x 7" red or pink foam craft
> 2" x 4" red or pink transparent film
> Permanent marker
> Low temperature glue gun

How to Make:
1. Follow instructions for making Reusable Patterns on page xv. Fold 3" x 13" piece of cardstock in half and make a pattern with hearts for the outside frame (see page 5). Set aside.
2. Make a reusable pattern for the two lens holders and set aside.
3. Make a reusable pattern for the lenses and set aside.
4. Unfold frame pattern and trace with pencil onto foam craft.

5. Trace two lens holder patterns onto foam craft.
6. Carefully cut frame and lens holders. (Adult help may come in handy here.)
7. Trace lenses onto transparent film with permanent marker and cut out.
8. With back side of frame up, glue film onto frame, making sure that each lens is centered and that it covers the entire opening.
9. Glue lens holders on top of lenses, again making sure the openings are centered.

Frame pattern

Lens pattern

Lens Holder pattern

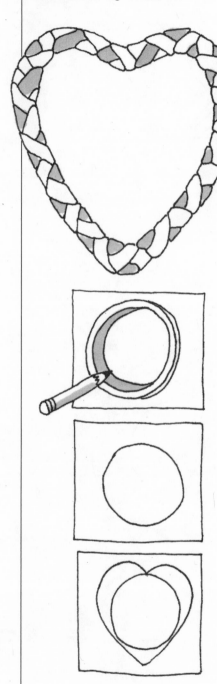

Woven Heart Jewelry

Use these pretty colors of Sculpey™ and weave them into a heart-shaped bracelet. You can easily convert the bracelet into a necklace with a 24" ribbon and a simple knot.

You Will Need:
   Sheet of paper
   Pencil
   An existing bracelet
   ½ ounce each red, pink, and purple Sculpey™
   Kitchen knife
   Glass baking dish
   Kitchen oven (preheated to 275°F)
   Ribbon streamers (optional)
   24" ribbon (for necklace)

How to Make a Woven Heart Bracelet:
1. Using your best-fitting round bracelet, draw a circle on a piece of paper on the inside of the bracelet.
2. Remove round bracelet and draw a heart around the outside of the circle.
3. Roll snake shapes of each color of Sculpey™ 12" long.

4. Weave the three colors together, then roll this to smooth the ridges.
5. Lay woven snake on top of your heart pattern.
6. Use knife to angle points at bottom of heart, and pinch together.
7. Smooth and soften the dip in the middle of the heart so it will be easy to wear.
8. Gently place the Sculpey™ heart onto the baking sheet at 275°F and bake in oven for 10 minutes.
9. Let cool before putting on your wrist.
10. For a more festive look, tie ribbon streamers on the point of the heart. Wave your arm and watch the colors fly.

How to Make a Woven Heart Necklace:
1. Find the center of the ribbon and hold the center under the inside peak of the heart.
2. Bring the loose ends of ribbon through the middle of the heart and down through the center of the ribbon.
3. Pull to tighten.
4. Tie the two loose ends together and wear as a necklace.

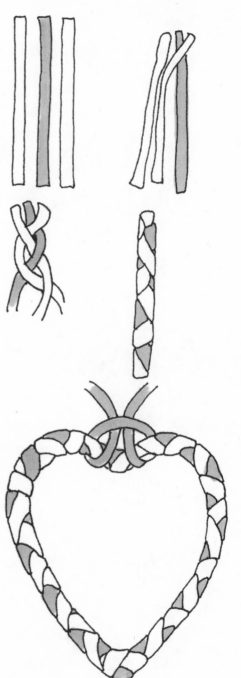

Frog Prince Pocket Clip

Don't let this guy out of your pocket or he may get kissed and turn into a prince. (He's much cuter as a frog.)

You Will Need:
  Large paper clip
  2" x 3" index card or cardboard
  1 ounce green Sculpey™
  ½ ounce yellow Sculpey™
  Small bits of white, black, and red Sculpey™
  Kitchen oven (preheated to 275°F)
  Glass baking dish

How to Make:
1. Paper clip the 2" x 3" piece of index card or cardboard. Lay the shorter side of the clip facing up.
2. Roll a ½" ball of green Sculpey™ and press to the bottom of the wire. Cover the entire bottom part of wire and mold to look like a frog head.
3. Roll two ¼" balls of green Sculpey™ and press to the lower sides of the first green shape and mold to look like frog hands.
4. Roll a ½" ball of yellow Sculpey™ and press to the top of the wire. Cover entire wire and mold to

look like a tall crown by making three points on the top.

5. Roll two small white balls about ⅛" round each. Press to frog face.

6. Roll two very small black balls about $^1/_{16}$" round each and press to whites of eyes.

7. Roll a skinny rope shape 1" long of red Sculpey™ and press to face for smiling mouth.

8. Place on baking dish and bake at 275°F for 12 minutes.

9. Remove from oven and let cool.

10. Gently slip off the cardboard and clip the Frog Prince on a pocket or a collar.

In that moment he was no longer a cold, fat, goggle-eyed frog, but a young Prince with handsome, friendly eyes.

—FROM "THE FROG PRINCE," BY THE BROTHERS GRIMM

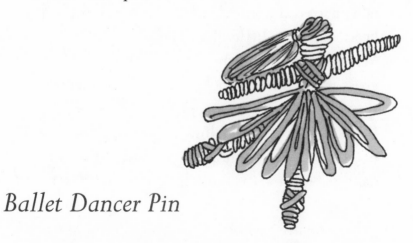

Ballet Dancer Pin

Make and wear a pin that reveals your love of ballet. This is similar to the way worry dolls are made, except the doll looks like she's in motion, and has no worries at all. Wrap thread tightly; there shouldn't be any gaps between strands.

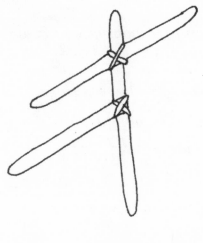

You Will Need:

    6 wooden craft sticks, 4" long
    Embroidery thread: pink, white, hair color,
      skin color
    1½" x 1½" piece cardboard
    Glue
    Scissors
    Jewelry pin

How to Make:

1. Begin by laying down one stick which will be the top of the head to the toe of the left foot.
2. Break a stick to be 3" long. Lay this stick diagonally across the first 1" down from the top of the head and put a little glue where they cross.
3. Wrap the intersection with pink thread in a crisscross pattern from back to front. Cut thread and spread glue over the wrapping.
4. Break a stick to be 2" long and lay it 2" up the left leg. This should be at an angle, parallel to the dancer's right arm. Put a little glue where they cross.
5. Wrap the intersection with pink thread in a crisscross pattern from back to front. Cut thread and spread glue over the wrapping. Let dry.
6. Wrap head and arms with two layers of skin-colored thread. Cut thread and spread the newly wrapped area with glue.

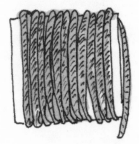

7. Wrap head a third and fourth time to create a more rounded shape and spread with a light layer of glue.

8. Wrap legs with two layers of white thread and spread with a light layer of glue.

9. Wrap toes with pink thread to make ballet slippers. Crisscross at the top to make laces. Spread with a light layer of glue.

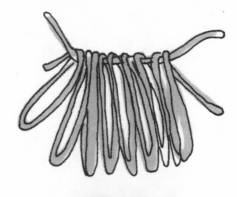

10. Wrap body with two layers of pink thread and cut end of thread. Wrap from waist to over shoulders in a crisscross pattern to make straps of tutu. Spread with a light layer of glue.

11. To make a skirt, wrap pink thread around 1½" x 1½" piece of cardboard. Tie through the top to attach all the loops and remove from cardboard.

12. Tie and glue skirt to waist of dancer. Spread with a light layer of glue and shape to make skirt stand out.

13. Wrap 1½" cardboard piece with hair-colored thread. Slide wrapped thread off the card and tie off ½" of it with a 2"-piece of thread to form the part of the hair that attaches to the head.

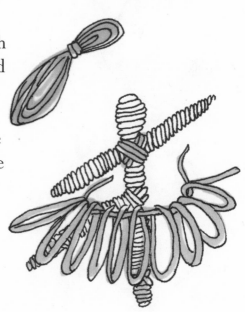

14. Glue hair to top of head and spread with a thin layer of glue. Let dancer dry about 20 minutes.

15. Glue jewelry pin to back of dancer.

Pocket Purse

Here's a small bag for quick errands. Felt comes in great colors and does not have to be hemmed. Add beads, jewels, or even embroidery around the edges.

You Will Need:
  2 pieces red felt, 6" square
  1 piece purple felt, 6" square
  Scissors
  Fabric glue
  Needle and embroidery thread (optional)
  36" heavy cord
  Beads and jewels

How to Make:
1. Follow instructions for making Reusable Patterns on page xv and use pattern on page 13.
2. Trace and cut red felt to make one whole red heart and one heart with no top to it.
3. Lay the heart with no top to it on top of full red heart.
4. Glue or stitch around the edges where the two layers meet. (If stitching, use blanket stitch.)
5. Glue or stitch shoulder cord to top sides of heart.

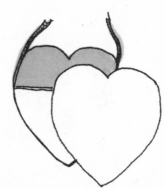

6. Make pattern for the top flap and cut from purple felt.

7. Decorate purple heart by gluing or stitching on beads and jewels.

8. Glue or stitch purple felt heart to top of red hearts. Attach only on the humps where the single layer of red meets the purple layer.

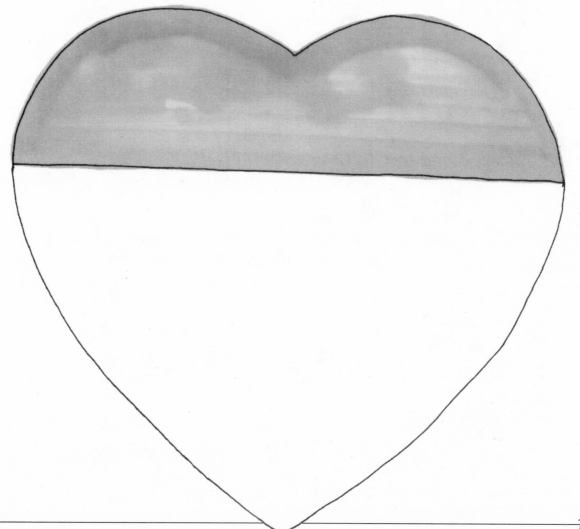

Daisy Hair Wreath

Your hair is the best place to wear flowers. Put on a fresh crown for the day and later preserve it in Silica Gel (available at craft stores) so you can wear it again.

You Will Need:
24 long-stemmed daisies
Scissors
Cutting surface
Kitchen knife
12" green string or thread
Silica Gel (optional)

How to Make:
1. Cut each of the flower's stems to 3" long.
2. Place a flower on the cutting surface and cut a 1"-long slit with the knife through the middle of the stem.
3. Repeat step 2 to all stems.
4. Stick the first flower stem through the slit of the second and pull the second stem all the way through the first.
5. Continue threading each stem until all the flowers are used. Hold the string of flowers around your

head. If necessary, make adjustments to the size by lengthening or shortening the connections.

6.   Tie the last stem to the first with the string or thread to make a hair wreath.

7.   Tie any loose stem ends with the green string or thread. Beautiful!

Button Slips

Tired of boring buttons or your button covers keep falling off? Slip into something artful—button slips. These are so easy you will have time to make and wear them in the same afternoon.

You Will Need:
   3" squares of foam craft
   Scissors
   Permanent markers
   Pencil
   X-acto knife
   Shirt with buttons

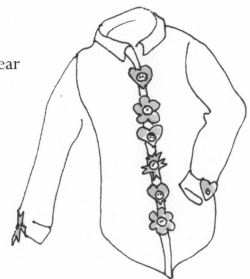

How to Make:

1. Trace and cut flowers and heart shapes of foam craft by following the instructions for Reusable Patterns on page xv.
2. Color and decorate slip shapes with permanent markers.
3. With pencil, mark the width of your button holes (from the shirt you are going to use) in the center of each slip.
4. Have an adult cut a slot with the X-acto knife in the center of each slip along the marking.
5. Put shirt on and button it. Slip button slips over each button and wear proudly.

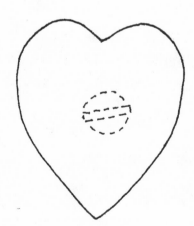

Love Potion

If you desire either romance or friendship to come
your way, mix up a batch of this stuff. Apply where
you would usually use cologne, and brace yourself.
(An easy alternative to this potion is to dab vanilla
extract behind your ear. Really!)

You Will Need:
  32 ounce Mason jar with lid
  Cheesecloth
  Scissors
  Cotton balls
  8 ounces mineral oil
  Fresh rose petals
  Non-iodized table salt
  1 cup marbles
  Masking tape
  Small funnel
  Perfume bottle with stopper

How to Make:
1. Place a piece of cheesecloth inside jar, such that
    the edges of cheesecloth hang out well over the
    top of the jar.

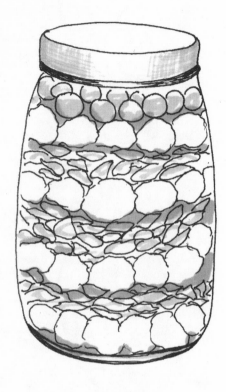

2   Trim cheesecloth leaving 2" extending over top of jar.

3.   Place a layer of cotton balls in bottom of jar and pour in about 3 tablespoons of oil.

4.   Layer 1" of rose petals on top of oil.

5.   Sprinkle with ⅛ teaspoon salt.

6.   Repeat steps 3–5 until jar is ¾ full. Make sure that the cotton balls cover all the petals at each layer. And make sure the cotton balls are saturated with oil. Finish with a final layer of cotton balls.

7.   Place a cup of marbles on top and press down.

8.   Fold the corners of cheesecloth inside the jar and put the lid on. Seal with masking tape and let sit for 48 hours.

9.   Open the jar and lift up the corners of the cheese cloth. Slowly pull cheese cloth up with one hand and press the marbles into the cotton balls as you lift, squeezing the oil into the jar.

10. Pour oil through the funnel into the perfume bottle. Always keep a stopper in the perfume bottle when not in use.

CHAPTER 2

Crafts from the Heart

These crafts all come from the heart and make wonderful friendship gifts. You're guaranteed to think good thoughts while you make them.

Conversation Heart Picture Frame

Surround your favorite photo with love.

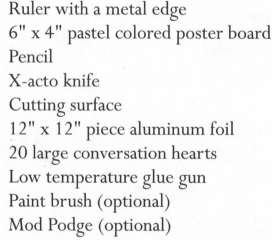

You Will Need:
> Ruler with a metal edge
> 6" x 4" pastel colored poster board
> Pencil
> X-acto knife
> Cutting surface
> 12" x 12" piece aluminum foil
> 20 large conversation hearts
> Low temperature glue gun
> Paint brush (optional)
> Mod Podge (optional)
> A favorite photo cut to 5½" x 3½"
> Scotch tape
> Picture frame hook or magnetic strip

How to Make:

1. Use the ruler to measure ½" inside the pastel colored poster board to draw a rectangle 5" x 3".
2. Have an adult cut out this rectangle with the X-acto knife, using the ruler's metal edge as a guide.

3. Place the aluminum foil in front of you as a work surface.

4. Lay the conversation hearts on the picture frame to decide how you want them arranged. It is best to place the hearts slightly turned to fit closely next to each other.

5. Glue the first heart in the middle of the top of the frame.

6. Continue gluing hearts around the frame until you have covered the frame. Let the glue dry.

7. If desired, paint with Mod Podge and let dry.

8. Turn the frame over and tape in your photo.

9. Glue the picture hook or magnetic strip to back of the frame.

It is a good idea to have as many best friends as you can.

—THE AUTHOR

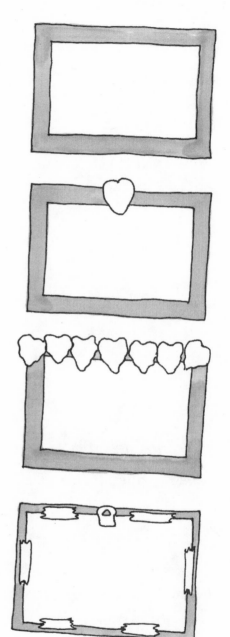

Pig and Mouse Puppets

Use these pig and mouse finger puppets to act out *Romeo and Juliet* or set them on your dresser to keep you company. The pig puppet will hold a tulip and your mousterpiece will hold a heart.

You Will Need:

    3¼" x 2½" pink foam craft (or construction paper)
    3¼" x 2½" gray foam craft (or construction paper)
    1" x ½" white foam craft (or construction paper)
    ½" x ½" red foam craft (or construction paper)
    Scissors
    Black, red, and green permanent markers
    Low temperature glue gun
    Pencil

How to Make:

1. Trace pig pattern on page 23 onto pink foam craft and cut out. Trace mouse pattern on page 23 onto gray foam craft and cut out. (See page xiv for tracing directions.)
2. Trace and cut out tulip in white foam craft. Trace and cut out heart in red foam craft.

3. Draw pig's face and ear marks and mouse's face and ear marks with black permanent marker.

4. Color tulip blossom red and stem green. Glue tulip to pig's middle, where its hands will be. Glue heart to mouse's middle, where its hands will be.

5. Draw pig hands and arms to look like they are holding the flower. Draw mouse's hands and arms to look like they are holding the heart.

6. Wrap pig puppet around your index finger and mark with pencil where to attach one side to the other.

7. With pig puppet off of your finger, glue sides together with glue gun. Repeat for mouse puppet.

Pig pattern *Mouse pattern*

23

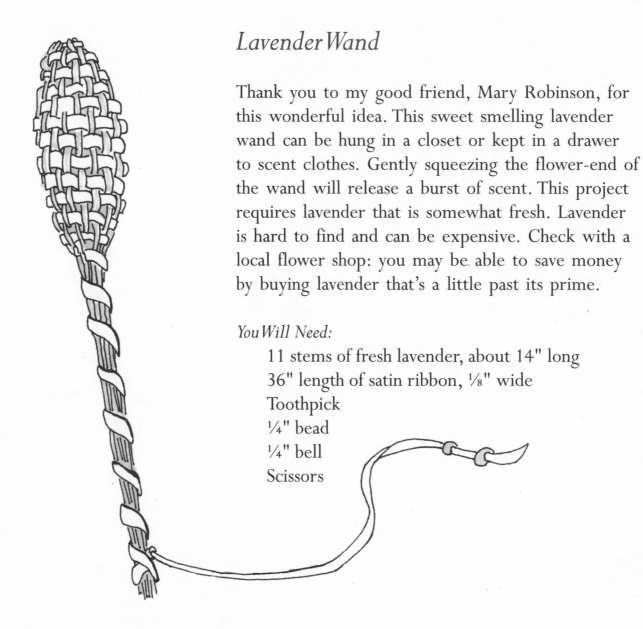

Lavender Wand

Thank you to my good friend, Mary Robinson, for this wonderful idea. This sweet smelling lavender wand can be hung in a closet or kept in a drawer to scent clothes. Gently squeezing the flower-end of the wand will release a burst of scent. This project requires lavender that is somewhat fresh. Lavender is hard to find and can be expensive. Check with a local flower shop: you may be able to save money by buying lavender that's a little past its prime.

You Will Need:
    11 stems of fresh lavender, about 14" long
    36" length of satin ribbon, ⅛" wide
    Toothpick
    ¼" bead
    ¼" bell
    Scissors

How to Make:

1. Bunch lavender together at the point where buds begin on the stem. Tie there with end of ribbon.

2. Bend stems out like tire spokes, then down, and over flowers. Stems should extend about 7" beyond the flowers.

3. Weave the ribbon over and under the first row of stems.

4. Bend stems down closer to flowers, and weave another row with ribbon. Rows should be woven tightly together. Use a toothpick to slide rows together as you weave.

5. Continue bending stems down closer to flowers while weaving additional rows. Pull ribbon so stems are tightly bound against the flowers.

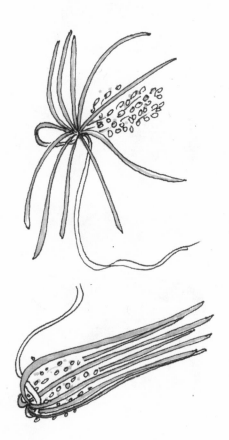

6. Continue weaving all the way to the flower tips.

7. Holding stems tightly together, continue wrapping ribbon around and down the stems.

8. Tie a knot and a bead at the end of the stems.

9. Leave about 6" of ribbon hanging from the end and tie on a bell.

10. As the flowers dry in the next few weeks, the ribbon on the stems will need to be tightened. Untie ribbon, tighten, and tie again.

Sand Heart Candle

I'll bet you haven't seen a sand candle that looks like this one. Simply use a heart tin to form its loving shape.

You Will Need:
> Plastic bowl, 5" diameter x 2" deep
> 1 cup sand, beach sand or purchased from craft
>   store
> ½ cup water
> Heart shaped baking tin, 3" diameter
> 6" candle wick
> Washer, ½" diameter or smaller
> Pencil
> 6 ounce wax
> Double boiler and water
> Newspapers, a few sheets
> Scissors

How to Make:
1. Fill bowl with 1 cup sand.
2. Pour in ½ cup water to wet sand.
3. Press bottom side of heart tin into wet sand. Pull out, leaving a heart shape. (If any of the sides fall

in, press tin in again. You may need to add a little more water to sand.)

4. Tie candle wick to washer and place in center of sand shaped heart.

5. Tie other end onto pencil and set on top of container. Tighten wick to be taut.

6. Ask an adult to help you carefully melt wax in a double boiler over low heat.

7. Pour melted wax into heart-shaped hole in sand. Position wick so that it is still in the center of the candle.

8. Let wax harden and cool, about 45 minutes.

9. Spread newspapers and carefully lift heart candle from container.

10. Dust off excess sand.

11. Trim wick with scissors.

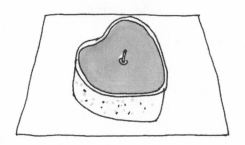

Rose Petal Drops

Rose petals never need to be thrown away. Turn them into delicate drops that can be hung to give off a lovely scent as you breeze by. Rose Petal Drops can be made from fresh or dried rose petals. The ideal petals are from roses that were cut two days before you make the drops. Collect fallen petals from rose gardens or from your local florist.

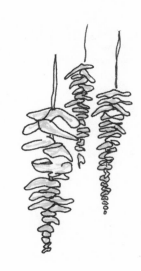

The rose is a rose,
And was always a rose,
But the theory now goes
That the apple's a rose,
And the pear is, and so's
The plum, I suppose.
The dear only knows
What will next prove a rose.
You, of course, are a rose—
But were always a rose.

—ROBERT FROST,
"THE ROSE FAMILY"

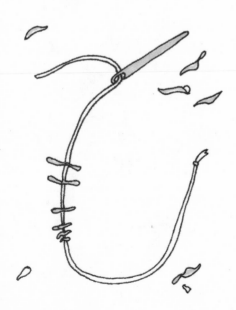

You Will Need:
Petals from 1 rose, per drop
Screen or paper towel
⅛" bead per drop
Thread
Large needle
3 green rose leaves

How to Make:
1. Take the petals from 1 rose and lay on a screen or paper towel for 2 days.
2. Tie bead at end of 12" of thread.
3. Thread the other end through needle.
4. Carefully poke the needle through the center of a rose petal to string onto the thread. Start with the smaller petals and finish with the largest ones.
5. String 3 green leaves at the top.
6. Adjust petals to look evenly spread along the thread.
7. Leave 6" of thread beyond the top; cut and tie in a loop.
8. Hang on wall, mantel, or tree for an aromatic decoration. Petals will shrink more as they continue to dry. Adjust them closer to each other on the thread as they dry.

Rose and Pearl Garland

Here's a delicate, twenty-four-inch decoration to swag on any tea table, over a doorway, even a mirror. Attach with tape or tacks.

You Will Need:
 Needle
 36" thread
 70 8 mm plastic pearls
 20 dried green rose leaves
 20 dried rose petals
 10 dried miniature rose buds

How to Make:
1. String a pearl and tie a knot to keep pearl in place.
2. String 6 more pearls.
3. String a leaf, a petal, a bud, a petal, and a leaf.
4. Repeat steps 2–3.
5. Continue to a length of about 2'.

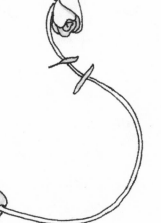

Symbol Thimble

Extend an offer of friendship to the Fairy World. It is well-known that if you leave just the right present out overnight, a fairy will come and enjoy it. So keep this offering on your nightstand or dresser to remind you of your tiny friends.

You Will Need:
  Scissors
  Magazine
  Thimble
  6" x 6" tissue
  6" ribbon

How to Make:
1. Cut out pictures of tiny hands from magazine.
2. Fill thimble with tiny hands.
3. Place thimble in center of tissue and bring the corners up.
4. Carefully tie with ribbon.

Land of kind dreams, where the mountains are blue, Where brownies are friendly and wishes come true. Through your green meadows they dance hand in hand—Little odd people of Buttercup Land.

—FROM AN EARLY
BEATRIX POTTER RHYME

CHAPTER 3

Sealed with a Kiss

Who doesn't like receiving love through the mail? The earliest known valentine was sent by the Duke of Orleans while he was imprisoned in the Tower of London in 1415. The Duchess liked it so much that she saved it. Lucky for us, because it is now on display in the British Library. The mail can be full of surprises. My favorite mail story is about

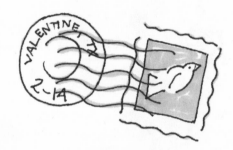

the ancient Egyptian queen, Cleopatra, who rolled herself up in a carpet and had herself delivered to Caesar, the Roman Emperor.

When sending valentines, love letters, and other artful messages, one clever touch is to have your mail sent through a romantically-named town. Address and stamp your mail. Write a note addressed to the Postmaster explaining that you would like your letter postmarked from that location. Put the note and your sealed and stamped mail in another envelope and send to the Postmaster of the appropriate town. These are some of my favorite places:

Angels Camp, CA 95222-9998
Loveland, CO 80538-9998
Loveville, MD 26656-9998
Loves Park, IL 61111-9998
Loving, TX 75851-9998
Valentine, TX 79854-9998
Valentines, VA 23887-9998

There are lots of ways to seal a love letter, but one of the best is with a real kiss. Apply red lipstick to your lips and actually kiss the back of the envelope!

Messenger of Love Dove

This is airmail at its finest. No postage is necessary for this one.

You Will Need:
8" x 8½" white paper
Ruler
Pencil
Scissors
Pen

How to Make:
1. Fold 8" x 8½" paper in half the long way to make it 4" x 8½".
2. With a pencil, draw a dove in flight on one side. Make a dot for the eye on the left, about 1" up and 1" from the edge. Draw a short line at an angle from left corner towards eye. Circle up and over the eye to make the top of the bird's head. Make a curved line from back of head to top of page, about 5½" from left. Draw three curved bumps down for the back of wing, stopping 1" before fold. Make a 2" straight line from bottom of wing to the right. Angle up to make the tail 2" from bottom.
3. Cut out dove and write a message on it in ink.
4. Fold wings down and send like a paper airplane.

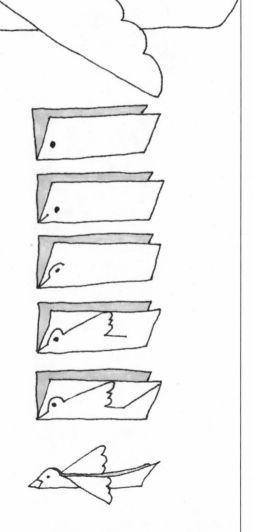

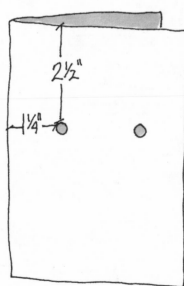

Surprise Package Card

Everyone loves a surprise, especially if it's from you!

You Will Need:
- 8½" x 6" white cardstock
- Hole punch or nail
- 24" white ribbon, ¼" wide
- 6" x 6" pink paper—stationery, construction paper, or origami paper
- Pencil
- Scissors
- Glue
- Photo cut to 2" square
- Pink marker

How to Make:
1. Fold cardstock in half and crease to make a 6" x 4¼" card.
2. Punch 2 holes with nail 2½" down from top on front of card, 1¼" from sides, and 1¾" apart.
3. Thread ribbon through holes with ends on top of card. Set aside.
4. Make a pattern of the surprise package shown on page 35 and trace it onto the pink paper.
5. Cut out the surprise package. Fold and crease as shown at dashed lines.

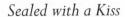

6. Glue surprise package on front of card, over the holes with ribbons coming out under each side. Let dry.

7. Unfold the surprise package and glue a 2" square photo inside.

8. Fold surprise package and tie ribbon to close.

9. Use the pink marker to write a message on the inside of card for the person you are going to give this to and sign your name.

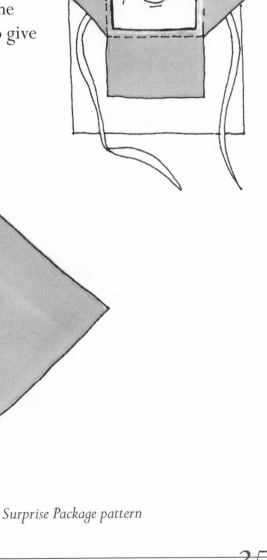

Surprise Package pattern

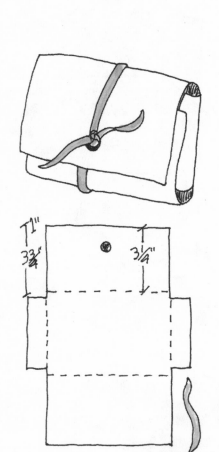

Envelope for Surprise Package Card

Make your surprise card even more surprising by making the envelope for it. Don't forget to say "I made it myself!"

You Will Need:
  8½" x 11" pink paper
  Pencil
  Ruler
  Hole punch or nail
  24" white ribbon, ¼" wide

How to Make:
1. Cut 1" x 3¾" rectangle off of each side of paper as shown.
2. Punch hole ¾" down from top, centered.
3. Fold over 1" on each side and crease.
4. Fold the bottom up 3¼" and crease.
5. Tie one end of the ribbon through hole leaving 3" of ribbon on the short side.
6. Insert card in envelope under folded flaps.
7. Wrap ribbon down, around the front and to the back again. Tie this end to the 3" end.
8. Address envelope and give to a friend.

Potted Tulip Pen

This tulip pen in its own flower-pot holder looks beautiful on a desk, and is perfect for writing out the cards in this chapter. "Crinkle paper" is a heavy scrunched-up craft paper that holds a shape well when molded.

You Will Need:
    8 pieces of 2" x 3" red crinkle paper
    4 pieces of 1" x 2" green crinkle paper
    Scissors
    Green ball point pen with cap (If you don't have a
        green pen, tightly wrap green construction
        paper around any pen and glue the paper on.)
    Thread
    Glue
    Low temperature glue gun
    3" clay flower pot
    3" square Styrofoam (available in flower shops or
        craft stores)

How to Make the Pen:
1. Make tulip petal pattern using pattern on page 38 and cut 8 red crinkle paper petals. (See pattern making instructions on page xiv.)

What do you get when you plant kisses? Two lips.

—HALEY WADSWORTH

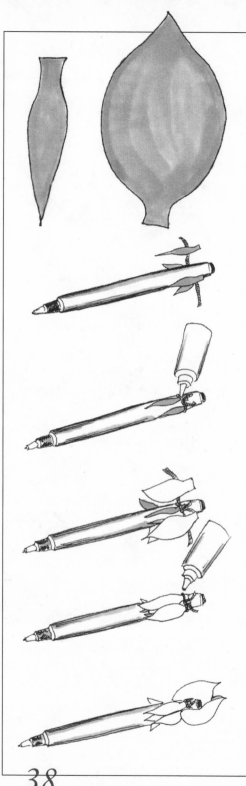

2. Make leaf pattern and cut 4 green crinkle paper leaves.

3. Point leaf tips down (upside-down). Tie 4 green leaves close to end of pen with thread. Spread thread with glue and let dry for 3 minutes.

4. Point tips of petals down (upside-down). Tie 4 red petals close to end of pen with thread. Spread thread with glue. Let dry for 3 minutes.

5. Repeat step 4.

6. Gently lift petals and leaves one at a time.

7. If petals don't come together in the center, glue the center three petals together.

How to Make the Pot:

1. Press 3" Styrofoam into bottom of pot.

2. With the pen cap on, glue and wrap the cap with 2" of green paper.

3. Make a hole in the center of Styrofoam by pressing the wrapped end of the pen 2" into it. Pull entire pen cap and paper out.

4. Remove wrapped paper and cap from pen, leaving cap glued inside the paper.

5. Spread hole with glue and stick wrapped paper with cap into it. Let sit to dry.

6. Cut slivers of green paper and glue to top of Styrofoam covering everything except the hole.

Heart of Gold Stamp and Sealing Wax

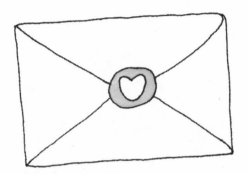

I have been intrigued with sealing wax since I was six years old. The only problem with young people using sealing wax unsupervised is that it can be a little dangerous. Here's a method I invented that is safe and even more creative. Variations on the stamp include pressing found objects into unbaked Sculpey™ pieces, or using a small rounded object to press in an initial. Remember, in making stamps with initials or words, they should be made in mirror image. To make an image really "pop," press outer surface of stamp on a permanent gold stamp pad. Then press into warm glue and the gold will appear on the recessed level of the wax causing the image to show up really well.

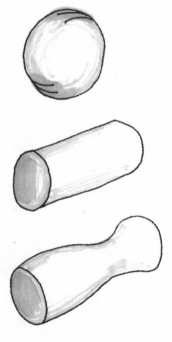

You Will Need:

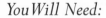

    1 ounce Sculpey™ (any color)
    Conversation heart
    Kitchen oven (preheated to 275°F)
    Glass baking dish
    Low temperature glue gun
    Colored glue stick (any color)
    Vaseline
    Envelope
    Permanent gold ink pad (optional)

39

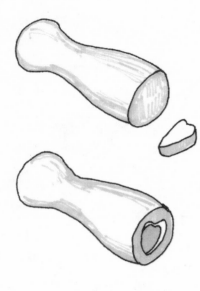

How to Make Heart Stamp:

1. Roll Sculpey™ into a 2" log shape.
2. Round one end and pinch in to make it easy to hold.
3. Flatten the other end by pressing on flat surface.
4. On the flattened end, press a conversation heart into the Sculpey™ ⅛" and remove.
5. Bake Sculpey™ on a glass baking dish in oven at 275°F for about 12 minutes.

How to Make Sealing Wax:

1. With glue gun, squeeze a spot of colored glue about ½" wide on the area that is to be sealed.
2. Spread a thin layer of Vaseline on the heart stamp.
3. Press stamp into warm glue and leave for 3 minutes, then remove.

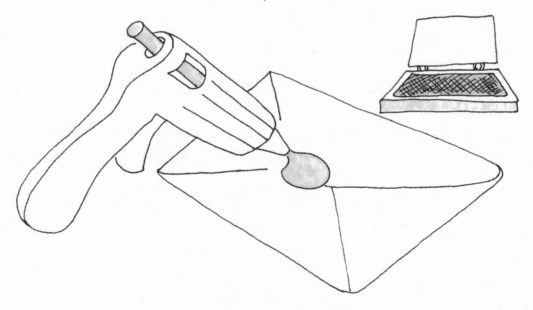

Thumb Print Seal

For a truly individual touch, try this idea.

You Will Need:
>   Your thumb
>   Red ink pad
>   Letter that needs a last minute touch

How to Make:
1.   Turn envelope so the back side is up.
2.   Press your thumb lightly on the ink pad, then press thumb once on paper at a slight angle to the left.
3.   Press thumb on ink once more and with your thumb turned at a right angle, press down on envelope to make a heart shape.

Lace Up a Perfect Heart

Hearts come in many shapes and sizes. Use the Perfect Heart instructions to make a heart that is flawlessly symmetrical. Then trim with lace that you make yourself.

You Will Need:

Reusable pattern for a Perfect Heart made from a 3" square and a 3" circle (follow Perfect Heart instructions on page xv.)

Reusable pattern for Perfect Heart made from a 4" square and a 4" circle

6" x 6" red paper

7" x 7" white paper

*Although I saw you
The day before yesterday,
And yesterday and today,
This much is true—
I want to see you tomorrow, too!*

—MASUHITO
(8TH CENTURY), "I LIKE YOU"

Compass
Scissors
Ruler
Pencil
Glue
8" x 10" piece of corrugated cardboard or
    Styrofoam
Push pin or large needle
Pen

How to Make:

1. Use the Perfect Heart pattern made from
    3" square and 3" circle and cut a heart from
    the red paper.
2. Use the Perfect Heart pattern made from
    4" square and 4" circle and cut a heart from
    the white paper.
3. Glue the red heart on top of the white heart to
    make it look like it has a white trim. Let dry.
4. Lay glued hearts on cardboard or Styrofoam.
5. With the push pin, punch in holes to create a lace
    pattern in the white trim.
6. Write a message on the red heart, slip it into an
    envelope, and mail.

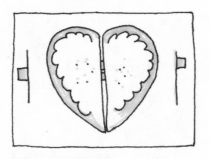

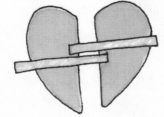

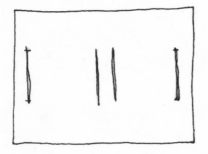

Beating Heart

This is a paper trick that can't be beat.

You Will Need:

    5" x 7" white cardstock
    X-acto knife
    3½" square white cardstock
    Pencil
    Ruler with metal edge
    Markers or crayons
    Lace and/or stickers (optional)
    Glue
    2 strips white cardstock, ½" x 4"

How to Make:

1. Have an adult help you cut four 2" slots in 5" x 7" cardstock with the X-acto knife where shown.
2. Make a heart 3½" wide on the 3½" square of cardstock and color or decorate.
3. Cut heart in half from peak to point.
4. Lay heart halves on white cardstock and mark where the 2 center slots line up.
5. Glue ½" x 4" strips of cardstock to the back of each heart-half and let dry.
6. Slide strips through slots, and pull strips to make the heart beat.

❦ CHAPTER 4 ❧

Tea Time

O, what better time of the day than tea time. Just a little something to hold us over until dinner. And a perfect time to catch up on chitchat and such. There is everything you need in this section to give a homemade tea party for your friends. Make all of these suggestions, or only a few, but don't forget the tea.

Use some of the crafts in the Sealed with a Kiss chapter for invitations. And you may wish to wear some of your creations from the Wearable Art section. You could even pick one of the crafts in this book for everyone to make at the party as part of the entertainment.

'Stay' is a charming word in a friend's vocabulary.

—LOUISA MAY ALCOTT

Cup of Kindness

This is a fun way to spread acts of beauty at a tea party, and it's always good to practice being a little kinder than is necessary.

You Will Need Before the Party:
 1 plain white tea cup and saucer
 Enamel paint
 Small paint brush
 Assorted hearts and beads
 Glitter glue
 Low temperature glue gun
 12" thin ribbon

You Will Need During the Party:
 One piece paper ½" x 3" and one pencil per guest

How to Make the Cup:

1. Paint the words "Cup of Kindness" on the cup and let dry.
2. Glue hearts and beads on tea cup and saucer's edge.
3. Paint petals around some of the beads to create flowers.
4. Make dots with glitter glue in chosen spots.
5. Tie ribbon on the cup's handle.

How to Play:

1. Give each guest a piece of paper and a pencil.
2. Each person is to write an act of kindness on the piece of paper. Explain that the act should be something a guest could do while at the party. Some suggestions for acts of kindness include: "give a pat on the back"; "pour a cup of tea"; "find something you like about the person to your left and tell them"; or "ask the person to your left what you can get for them."
3. Fold the papers and mix them up in the cup.
4. Each guest picks one piece of paper. The act of kindness is to be performed by the guest who picks it for the person on their left.

No act of kindness no matter how small is ever wasted.

—from "The Lion and the Mouse" by Aesop

Tea Candle

Give a little tea light a makeover! You may want to keep a few of these candles with aluminum bases on hand. They are great for party favors or for lighting up a tea table.

You Will Need:
>   Tea light
>   ½ ounce white Sculpey™ rolled into ball
>   1 ounce purple Sculpey™ rolled into ball
>   Rolling pin
>   Kitchen oven (preheated to 275°F)

How to Make:

1.   Gently remove candle from aluminum holder and set aside.
2.   Use the rolling pin to flatten the ball of white Sculpey™ into a piece 1" square. Cut four ½" x ½" hearts out of this and set aside.
3.   Use the rolling pin to flatten the ball of purple Sculpey™ into a long, skinny rectangle ¾" x 5".
4.   Apply purple rectangle to the outside of the aluminum holder.
5.   Trim excess purple and roll it into a ball.
6.   With excess purple, make a flat circle shape

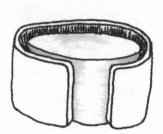

1½" diameter and apply to the bottom of holder. Use fingertips to mold bottom circle smoothly to the sides. Review your handiwork and smooth where necessary.

7. With clean hands, press the white hearts into the purple sides. Roll or flatten slightly.
8. Bake at 275°F for about 15 minutes. Remove from oven and let cool.
9. Place candle back into the holder and it is ready to be given away or placed on a tea table.

Petal Place Card

Create delicate papers with naturally dried petals. You can also take this same idea and make gift tags, invitations, or greeting cards.

You Will Need:
Rose petals
Paper towel or drying screen
Pink construction paper, 3" x 2"
White construction paper, ¾" square
Glue

How to Make:
1. Collect several fallen rose petals and place on screen or paper towel to dry for 1 week. It's fine

49

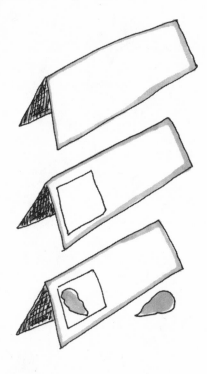

if petals are not pressed, they will just have a more natural look.

2. Fold pink paper in half, vertically, and crease with fingers. The crease is the top and the open ends are the bottom.

3. Choose which side will be the front. Glue white square to the left on front of pink card and let dry.

4. Print guest's name to the right of the white square.

5. Decide which two rose petals will work best to form a heart and glue these to the white square one at a time.

6. Place at guest's spot at the table.

Red Hot Cinnamon Tea

Add a little heat to your homemade tea by tossing in a few red hots. Let your guests toss in their own. Serves four.

You Will Need:
    6 cups water in pan with lid
    1 stick cinnamon
    2 tablespoons loose tea
    Piece of cheesecloth or tea strainer
    Teapot
    Small plate or bowl of red hots

How to Make:

1. Break the cinnamon stick into 4 pieces and place in the pan of water. With an adult's help, bring to a boil.
2. Add loose tea leaves, and cover the pan. Remove from heat and let sit for 5 minutes.
3. With adult help, pour the hot liquid into a teapot while using tea strainer or cheesecloth to catch the leaves and cinnamon stick pieces (which can then be discarded).

How to Serve:

1. Pour each guest a cup of tea.
2. Pass around the red hots, and suggest that each guest drop 3 into their cups.

> *Each friend represents a world in us, a world possibly not born until they arrive, and it is only by this meeting that a new world is born.*
>
> —ANAIS NIN

Cinnamon Stick Honey Dips

Much more whimsical than using a spoon, these cinnamon sticks are very useful. Serves four.

You Will Need:
    4 cinnamon sticks
    Bowl of honey
    Cups of tea

How to Make:

1. Pass around the cinnamon sticks and show your guests how to use them by dipping one in the honey and twirling it around before placing the stick in your tea cup.
2. Stir to add a sweet cinnamon flavor to the tea.

Cherry Vanilla Scones

The best choice to serve at a tea is not muffins or cookies, but scones. Scones are not too sweet, not too plain, but just right. This recipe makes six servings.

You Will Need:

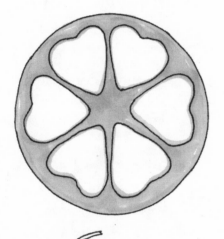

    6 greased heart tins or 1 greased baking sheet
    Mixing bowl
    Fork
    2 cups flour
    Pinch of salt
    2½ teaspoons baking powder
    ¼ cup powdered sugar, plus a little extra for
        tops of scones
    6 tablespoons cold butter cut into ¼" pieces, plus
        a little extra for greasing tins
    1 egg
    ½ cup milk
    Dash of vanilla extract

¾ cup pitted, chopped, dried cherries
Kitchen knife
Kitchen oven (preheated to 425°F)

How to Make Batter:
1. Combine the flour, salt, baking powder, and sugar in mixing bowl. Stir with a fork to mix well.
2. Add butter to flour mixture and cut with fork. Use fingertips and knead butter into the flour. Mixture should look like coarse bread crumbs.
3. In a small mixing bowl, break egg, beat with fork, and add ½ cup milk.
4. Add a dash of vanilla to liquid and beat with fork.
5. Combine egg and milk mixture with flour mixture and beat, about 50 strokes.
6. Fold in cherries and mix well, about 8 strokes.

How to Bake the Scones:
1. Divide dough into 6 tins or shape 6 hearts on baking sheet.
2. Sprinkle the top of each scone with sugar.
3. With an adult's help, place in oven and bake for 15 minutes, or until tops are golden brown.
4. Remove from oven and let cool.
5. Remove scones from tins by running a dull knife between scone and tin. Gently turn over tin with one hand and catch the scone with the other.

Peach Rose Jam

Spread this fresh, fruity-flowery joy on toast or scones for a yummy summertime treat. Rose water can be purchased at pharmacies or ethnic markets, labeled as Fluid Rose Soluble, or you can make it yourself (see following recipe).

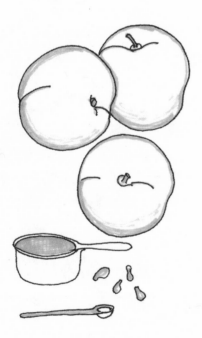

You Will Need:
   3 medium peaches, fresh
   Fork
   Bowl
   ⅓ cup sugar
   ⅛ teaspoon rose water
   4 crystallized rose petals
   Jam jar with lid

How to Make:
1. Wash, peel, and pit peaches. Mash with a fork.
2. Add sugar, rose water, and rose petals to mashed peaches. Mix until well blended.
3. Let mixture sit for 30 minutes until sugar dissolves.
4. Store in jam jar and keep in refrigerator. Jam will keep for 1 week.

Rose Water

Use this in recipes and crafts, or dab it behind your ears. Bottled rose water should keep for up to two weeks if the stopper fits tightly.

You Will Need:
   ½ cup water
   Saucepan
   4 cups rose petals
   Small funnel
   3 ounce bottle (or larger) with a stopper
   12" piece of cheesecloth

How to Make:
1. With an adult's help, boil water in uncovered saucepan.
2. Add rose petals and stir for 2 minutes.
3. Remove from heat and let cool completely.
4. Place the funnel in mouth of bottle.
5. Fold cheesecloth to be a 6" square and lay on top of funnel, pushing cloth into the funnel slightly.
6. Strain the water through the cheesecloth keeping rose petals in the cloth.
7. Squeeze out any extra liquid and discard petals.

Crystallized Rose Petals

When making this recipe, it seems almost as if you are creating fine jewels, not a yummy treat. I just like the way the petals look after they have been crystallized. They may be eaten just as is or used to decorate other dishes, or they can be strung to make the Edible Garland in the recipe after this one.

You Will Need:
  Petals from one fresh rose
  1 egg white in a bowl
  Fork
  Small paint brush
  ¼ cup sugar, on a plate
  Paper towels

How to Make:
1. Gently wash and rinse rose petals.
2. Lay clean rose petals on paper towel and pat dry.
3. Using the fork, beat the egg white until frothy.
4. Brush a rose petal on both sides with the egg white.
5. Gently dip the petal in the sugar, coating both sides. Use your fingers to sprinkle sugar on areas

that still need sugar, then lay petal on paper towel
to dry.

6. Repeat steps 4–5 for the other petals.
7. Store Crystallized Rose Petals in an airtight con-
    tainer. They will last about 1 week.

Edible Garland

This should really be called Giggly Edible Garland,
because you will surely laugh when you eat it. It does
seem a little silly. Please laugh with your mouth
closed.

You Will Need:
>   Fresh blueberries, about 42
>   Pointed wooden craft stick, same diameter as
>   licorice
>   Crystallized Rose Petals, about 8 roses-worth
>   Skinny red licorice lace, 36" long

How to Make:
1. Wash and dry blueberries.
2. Poke a hole all the way through each blueberry
    and through each petal with the craft stick.

3. Tie a knot at one end of licorice string and slide 3 petals to the knot, then string 7 blueberries, sliding them down until they touch the petals.

4. Continue to string 3 rose petals followed by 7 blueberries until you reach desired length or all materials are gone.

5. Drape your garland loosely around the base of cakes, or rope it around a Strawberry Castle instead of the Blueberry Moat (see following recipe). Or just eat it.

Strawberry Castle with Blueberry Moat

The result of this delicious recipe looks like a flaming red castle with a flowing blue moat. *And* you can eat it!

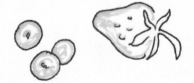

You Will Need:
　　1 pineapple
　　Large round plate
　　1 basket strawberries, washed, with leaves on

Toothpicks
Deep bowl
Hand mixer
1 pint whipping cream
2 tablespoons sugar
⅛ teaspoon vanilla extract
1 basket blueberries, washed

How to Make:

1. Ask an adult to help you clean and cut the pine-apple into a rounded cone shape and place it on the plate.

2. The first row of strawberries starts at the base of the pineapple. Stick a toothpick through a large strawberry and into the base. Encircle the pine-apple with large strawberries; leaves should be pointing down.

3. Moving up the pineapple, build a second row of slightly smaller strawberries, leaves pointing upwards.

4. Continue all the way up to the top of the pine-apple using smaller berries each time; leaves should alternate up and down.

5. In deep bowl, combine whipping cream and sugar. Beat with mixer until soft peaks form in the cream; the tips of the peaks should curl when you lift up the mixer.

6. Add vanilla and mix a few times to combine.
7. Spoon out a puffy circle of whipped cream around the base of your Strawberry Castle.
8. Lay washed blueberries on top of the whipped cream, and voilá—it's time to storm the castle with a spoon!

When the meadows laugh with lively green,
and the grasshopper laughs in the merry scene;
When Mary, and Susan, and Emily
With their sweet round mouths sing, "Ha, Ha, He!"
When the painted birds laugh in the shade,
Where our table with cherries and nuts is spread:
Come live, and be merry, and join with me,
To sing the sweet chorus of "Ha, Ha, He!"

—William Blake,
"Laughing Song"

CHAPTER 5

Sweet Dreams

Ah, wrapping up the day! Squeeze a little sweetness into every last moment by bathing with a heart, sneaking a chocolate onto someone's pillow, and writing down your deepest thoughts. Wink, blink, and nod. Hear the fairies whisper "Sweet dreams," sleep tight, and don't forget to blow out the candlelight.

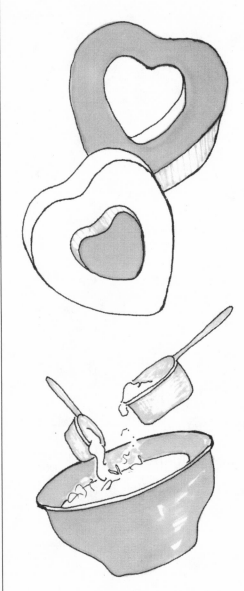

Two-Hearts-Are-Better-Than-One Soap

These are easy and satisfying to make. Use as decoration, or suds up some good clean fun. Makes two.

You Will Need:
  Wax paper
  ¼ cup water
  1½ cup soap flakes
  2 mixing bowls
  Spoon
  2 heart-shaped baking tins, 4" in diameter
  Red food coloring
  1½" heart-shaped cookie cutter
  2 tablespoons rose water (see page 55)

How to Make:
1. Prepare a work surface by spreading a sheet of wax paper.
2. Combine ⅛ cup water, 1 tablespoon rose water, and ¾ cup soap flakes in mixing bowl. Stir with spoon.
3. Turn the mixture onto the wax paper and knead for 1 minute.
4. Press mixture into one heart-shaped muffin tin.

Remove excess from the top by levelling with your finger. Set excess mixture aside.

5. Combine ⅛ cup water, ¾ cup soap flakes, 1 tablespoon rose water, and ⅛ teaspoon of red food coloring in second mixing bowl. Then repeat steps 3 and 4.

6. Knead both batches of excess mixture together to form a marbled ball.

7. Flatten marbled ball until 1" thick and press out a heart with cookie cutter.

8. Remove excess mixture from around cutter, roll it into a ball, and repeat step 7.

9. Let all of your new hearts set for 2 hours.

10. When set, turn over muffin tin and tap gently on bottom to remove heart.

11. Rub rose water on cookie cutter heart and press onto larger heart to stick them together.

12. Repeat steps 10 and 11. Allow your creation to dry carefully for one week.

Love is, above all, the gift of oneself.

—Jean Anouilh

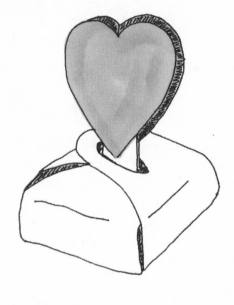

Paper Heart Box

Have you ever stayed at a hotel where they turn your bed down and place chocolates on the pillow? You can do this at home for friends and family. It's a great midnight snack that guarantees sweet dreams. It's especially sweet to deliver the next two activities in secret.

You Will Need:

> 8" x 6½" white cardstock (preferably coated on one side)
>
> Pencil
>
> Scissors
>
> X-acto knife
>
> Red permanent marker

How to Make:

1. Trace Heart Box pattern on page 66 onto white cardstock and cut. (See tracing directions on page xiv.)
2. Have an adult cut the two slots in A and B with an X-acto knife.
3. Draw the heart points to both ends, on both sides of the paper. To do this, draw at an angle down and towards the center.

4. Color in with red permanent marker and let dry.
5. With the coated side of paper down and uncoated side up, fold up and crease the sides of the box where dashed lines show.
6. Fold and crease the four square corner flaps.
7. Fold and crease the sides to the hearts. (This would be the time to place a chocolate inside the box.)
8. Bring the two folded hearts up touching together.
9. Carefully press hearts down into the box. Slip the slot of A over the two hearts. Repeat with the other slitted side.
10. Open the flaps of both hearts.
11. Secretly place your creation on a loved-one's pillow just before they turn in.

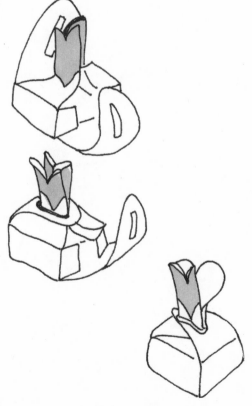

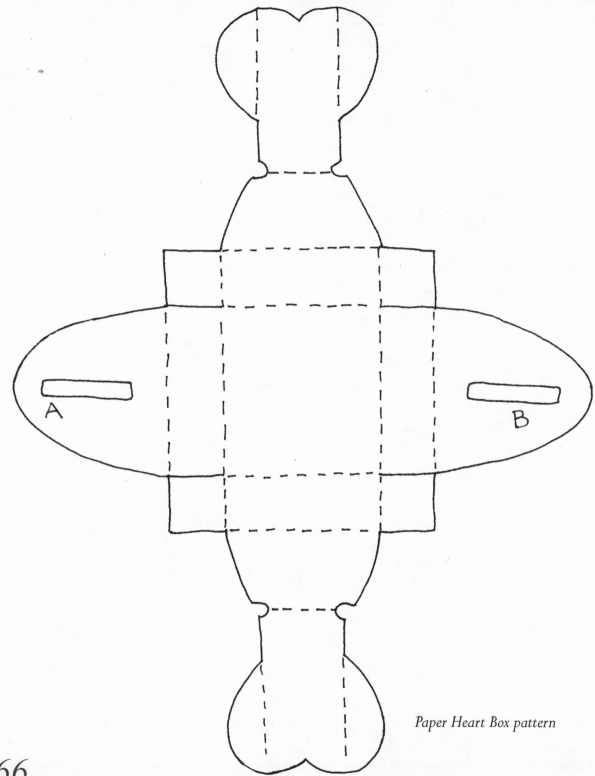

Paper Heart Box pattern

Heart Truffles

These professional-looking chocolates go perfectly with the Paper Heart Box.

You Will Need:
>   6 ounces chocolate chips
>   Double boiler
>   1 egg yolk
>   6 tablespoons softened butter
>   ⅔ cup powdered sugar
>   1 teaspoon vanilla extract
>   ¼ cup chopped walnuts
>   Cocoa powder
>   Tissue or foils for wrapping

How to Make:
1. With an adult's help, melt chocolate chips in a double boiler. Stir, remove from heat and let cool slightly.
2. Cream egg yolk and butter together.
3. Slowly add sugar to egg and butter mixture and mix well.
4. Pour the cooled chocolate into sugar mixture.
5. Add vanilla and nuts, and stir until well blended.
6. Refrigerate until firm enough to hold a shape.

7. Shape into small 1½" x ½" hearts.
8. Press one side of hearts into the cocoa.
9. Refrigerate until ready to use, then wrap with foil and place inside the Paper Heart Box.

Butterfly Kisses

Most of us know that a fluttery butterfly kiss happens when two people stand really close, eye to eye in fact, and bat their eyelashes together. Less well known is this sweet surprise with the same name. Just before your admired one goes to bed, slip into their room, turn down the covers, place a Butterfly Kiss on the pillow, and fly away.

You Will Need:
    1 Hershey Kiss
    2½" square of gold foil paper
    Red paint pen
    Glue

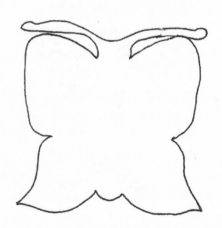

Butterfly pattern

How to Make:
1. Trace pattern and cut butterfly from gold foil paper.
2. Decorate with red paint pen.
3. Glue back of butterfly to the little paper strip that sticks out of the Kiss' wrapper.

Window Box

This unusual craft comes from artist and writer Robin Oldham. During the day, light will come through this softly painted box like a stained glass window and little mementos will show up as nice silhouettes. At night, if you want to see their outlines, ask an adult to set a lit candle behind the box.

You Will Need:
>   Clear plastic compartment or utility box
>   Acrylic paints
>   Brush
>   Tiny mementos (dried flower, ticket stub,
>   pretty shell)

How to Make:

1. Lightly paint compartment squares with the different colors and let dry.
2. Add tiny mementos to some of the compartments and set on window sill.

Tissue Candle

When you light these lovely luminaries they will glow softly through your doves, flowers, hearts, or geometric cut-outs.

You Will Need:
Different colored tissue papers
Scissors
2 tablespoons glue
2 tablespoons water
Mixing bowl
Plain, clear glass candle holder with 2"-tall
    votive candle

How to Make:
1. Trace patterns and cut shapes from tissue. Set aside.
2. Mix glue and water in bowl.
3. Paint mixture on glass.
4. Gently lay tissue shapes on glass and let dry.

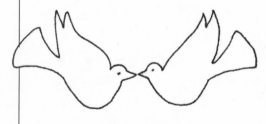

Heaven Scent

Add a sweet-smelling touch of heaven to your night. Place Heaven Scent next to your bedside to watch over you while you sleep.

You Will Need:
> Gold sparkle pipe cleaner
> Scissors
> 6" square fabric in small print
> Needle and thread
> 1 cotton ball
> 1 tablespoon potpourri or sweet-smelling mixed
>   herbs and flowers like basil, blue violet,
>   and rose
> Fabric glue
> 1 conversation heart or handmade heart

How to Make:
1. Cut pipe cleaner in half.
2. Bend one-half of pipe cleaner into a heart shape.
3. Twist the second half of pipe cleaner from the point of the heart, to the peak of the heart, and beyond.
4. Make a circle shape with the piece that is extending

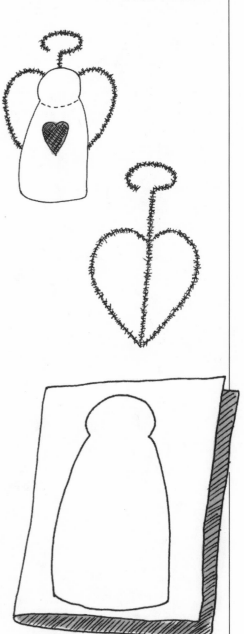

Heaven Scent Angel pattern

71

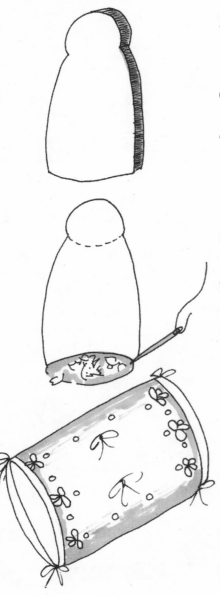

past the top of the heart. This will be the halo. Set halo and wings aside.

5. Fold cloth in half and cut two pieces in the shape of an angel. (See pattern making instructions on page xiv.)

6. Lay one piece of fabric down with back side of fabric facing up.

7. Lay second piece of fabric on top of this with right side up. Make small stitches close to the outside edge of the head of the angel. Stuff head with the cotton ball.

8. Stitch down one side of angel and then the other side.

9. Fill body of angel with herbs and stitch bottom closed.

10. Lay wings and halo on back of angel and attach with fabric glue at heart point and peak. Let dry.

11. Turn angel over, glue heart to center, and let dry.

Pamper Pillow

Rest and relax with a Pamper Pillow. It's just the right weight and can be cooled in the refrigerator to refresh tired eyes.

You Will Need:

　　1 scarf, 12" square
　　Fabric glue
　　½ cup flax seed
　　¼ cup dried rose petals
　　Ribbons and beads

How to Make:

1.　Glue scarf along bottom edge. Continue to glue 4" up from the bottom along the right and left sides.

2.　Fold the bottom 4" of scarf up to meet 4" of unglued area, and press together. Let dry.

3.　Mix together flax seeds and rose petals.

4.　Through the open side, fill pillow with seed mixture.

5.　Glue along edge just inside the opening, pinch shut, and let dry.

6.　Glue scarf along all four edges that face up around the enclosed seed mixture. Fold this area up onto the last 4" of scarf. Press and let dry.

7.　Glue all openings to seal, and let dry.

8.　Glue beads and ribbons on only one face of pillow; leave the rest of the pillow free of decoration so that it will be smooth for placing on your eyes.

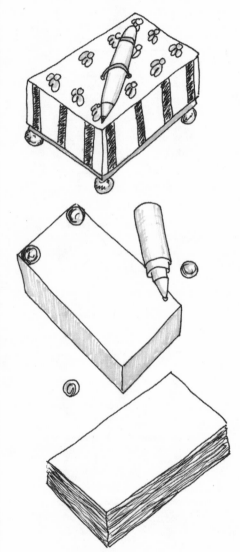

Dream Keeper

When you have something you want to remember, whether it is a dream, a wish, a poem, or something that happened during your day, open up your Dream Keeper. Use one of the cards and write down your thoughts.

Part of the fun of the Dream Keeper is that it is unstructured. There is no beginning and no end. You can shuffle back and forth from card to card and even add something to what you wrote three days ago. Feel free to use other pens, watercolors, or stickers to make the cards uniquely your own.

You Will Need:
> Checkbook box or similar box
> 4 round beads, ¼" diameter
> Glue
> Cardstock
> Scissors
> Ruler
> Wrapping or origami paper
> Nail
> 2" thin, silver, elastic thread
> Writing utensil

How to Make:

1. Glue a bead to each corner of the bottom of box to make feet, and let dry.

2. Cut 30 pieces of cardstock to about 2¾" x 6" and lay inside box.

3. Decorate the lid of checkbook box with pretty paper. (The bottom of the box does not have to be covered.)

4. Use a small nail to punch two holes ¼" apart through the center of the lid.

5. Poke each end of the silver elastic thread through the holes and tie in a knot on backside of lid.

6. Place your favorite writing instrument under the elastic and you are ready to record your wishes, dreams, or diary entries.

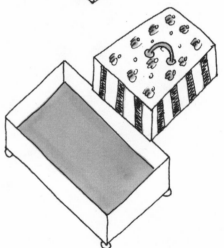

The sun is down!
There is peace in nature, peace in my heart!
The evening is so light!
We sail!
The night is clear! We sail!

—Hans Christian Andersen,
from "A Poet's Bazaar"

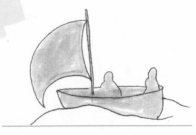

*I've dreamt in my life dreams that have
stayed with me ever
after, and changed my ideas. They've gone
through and through me like wine through water,
and altered the color
of my mind.*

—Emily Bronte

More fun books you may enjoy…

THE MUDPIES ACTIVITY BOOK
Recipes for Invention
Nancy Blakey

Based on materials you can easily find around the house, this popular sourcebook includes a hurricane in a bottle, things to do with pumpkins, a do-it-yourself radio show, and more.
• Ages 2 to 12, 144 pages, paperback

MORE MUDPIES
101 Alternatives to Television
Nancy Blakey

Continuing in the fine Mudpies tradition, here's more creative fun based on simple materials ("Love Medicine") or no materials at all ("Island Hippety-Hop").
• Ages 2 to 12, 144 pages, paperback

100 WONDERFUL THINGS TO KEEP KIDS BUSY AND HAVING FUN
Pam Schiller and Joan Rossano

This book lives up to its title: 100 simple activities that require no expertise.
• Ages 3 to 7, 96 pages, paperback

PRETEND SOUP…AND OTHER REAL RECIPES
A Cookbook for Preschoolers & Up
Mollie Katzen and Ann Henderson

19 vegetarian recipes (no gimmicky kids' food!) by a renowned cookbook author and a preschool teacher.
• Ages 3 to 8, 96 pages, hardcover

"What makes this book so alluring is the art—bright whimsical animals—and the two sets of instructions. One set is for adults. The other set is for the small chefs, containing bright, clear and easy-to-follow graphics. They don't even need to be able to read!" —Washington Post

Fairies from A to Z
A Fairy Box Book
Adrienne Keith, Illustrations by Wendy Wallin Malinow

Colorful and magical, this little book invites you into the whimsical world of fairies—and comes complete with a fold-up fairy house for inviting tiny guests to stay awhile.

• Ages 3 and up, 48 pages, hardcover

Fairies: Celebrations from Season to Season
Adrienne Keith, Illustrations by Wendy Wallin Malinow

This time the fairies share with lucky readers their secret festivals, games, recipes and crafts. And of course there's a new fairy box inside.

• Ages 3 and up, 32 pages, hardcover

Amelia's Notebook
Marissa Moss

Reading this book is like peeking at a friend's private journal, and it looks like one, too! With real kid appeal.

• Ages 7 and up, 32 pages, hardcover

"I liked this book because it was different than other books. I keep a journal too and I also tape things in it. I think you should make a sequel that is longer."—Laura Vermeulen, Age 11

For more information, or to order, call the publisher at the number below. We accept VISA MasterCard, and American Express. You may also wish to write for our free catalog of books, posters, and audiotapes for kids and their grown-ups.

Tricycle Press
P.O. Box 7123
Berkeley, CA 94707
1-800-841-BOOK